THE GERM

How to Talk to Children about Racism and Diversity

By: Deidra A. Sorrell, Ed.D, NCC, LPC, ACS

Illustrated by: Carizza Losbanos

Published by: Synergy Wellness Therapeutic Services LLC

Printed by: Createspace

ISBN-13: 978-1522804383

Printed in the United States of America

First print December 2015

Second print, December 2017

This story is dedicated to the memory of:

Sandra Bland
Freddy Gray
Walter Scott
Mike Brown
Tamir Rice
Eric Garner
Rekia Boyd
John Crawford
Miriam Carey
Oscar Grant
Sean Bell
Amadou Diallo
Laquan McDonald

And all of the other people who have been
unwarrantedly injured or
killed before due process was served.

One day I was watching the news with my family. Suddenly the news reported that man in my city was hurt by a police officer. Some people said that the man was running from the police officer. Other people said that the man was then shot by the police officer. Many people did not know what really happened.

I suddenly became worried. I was scared because that man was the same color as my daddy and my little brother Jacob. The man kind of looked like my next door neighbor, Mr. Slim. My Mommy told me not to worry as she turned off the T.V.

I could not stop worrying as I brushed my teeth. I worried more as I took my bath. I worried even more as it was time for me to go to bed. My skin is brown like the man who was hurt. Would someone hurt me while I am on my way to school? Would someone hit my brother? Would someone hurt my daddy as he comes home from work? Would someone hurt my Mommy or my next door neighbor, Mr. Slim?

As my Mommy pulled out a story for us to read before bed, I asked her, "Did a raisin hurt that man on T.V.?" My Mommy looked puzzled and replied, "Of course not Ruby". "Why did daddy say that the man was hurt because of a raisin?" I asked. Mommy took a deep breath and explained. "Daddy said that the reason the man was hurt was because of racism".

"What is Racism?" I asked. "Racism is when certain people think a skin color is bad, based on their own ignorance", Mommy replied. "Are some people this way to black people"? I asked.
"Yes, unfortunately that is an example, but every skin color is beautiful and special in God's eyes. We never want to change our God given skin color, but change the ignorance of the people who believe that a certain skin color is better than another", Mommy replied.

"But I am not mean to people with different skin colors," I said.
"I know some people with white skin who are very nice," I said.
"My friend Caden has white skin and he is a good friend and our neighbor Ms. Parker has white skin and she always brings us yummy snicker doodles," I said. I was so confused!!!

"I think racism is like a germ," Mommy continued. "Like a cold or the flu?" I asked. "Sort of," Mommy replied. "Some people have the germ and some people do not," Mommy said. "How do you get the germ?" I asked. "This germ comes from not knowing much about people who are different," Mommy said. "Remember when Raul moved down the street?" Mommy asked.

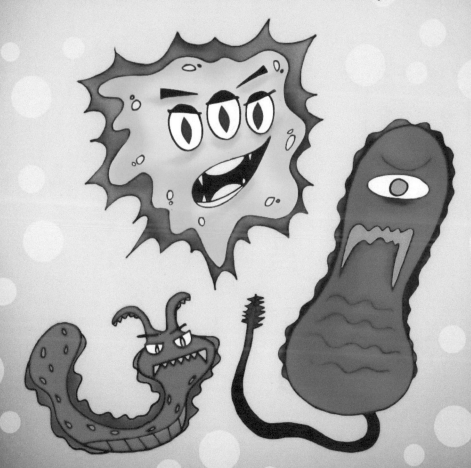

I thought about Raul, who is from Mexico, who moved down the street from me last year. Raul speaks English and Spanish. When I first met Raul, I was afraid because he spoke a different language that I did not understand. When I got to know Raul, I saw that he and I were more alike than we were different. "Yes, Mommy, we are such good friends after I got to know him," I said.

"People who have the germ have been taught to believe that they are better than others because their skin is a certain color," Mommy said. "But, when we really get to know one another, we find out that we may look different, but we are all equal," Mommy said.

"Do all the police have the germ?" I asked. "Of course not, there are many great police officers that protect us and help us. Just like Mr. Ramsey, the police officer who helps your school," Mommy said. "Yes, Mr. Ramsey is the best!" I exclaimed.

"Can black people have the germ against other black people?"
I asked. Mommy thought about it for a while. "I suppose some
black people have bought into the belief that certain brown skin
colors are better than others," Mommy said. "That sounds like my
friend Janay who said that dark skinned boys are ugly," I replied.
"Well that was not a nice thing for Janay to say," Mommy said.

"The germ is when people believe that certain skin colors are not pretty, cute or smart. But you know that people of all skin colors can be totally awesome!" Mommy said. "Aww, Mommy, nobody says totally awesome," I said with a laugh.

"Mommy, you give us medicine for a cold, but how does a person get rid of the germ?" I asked. "I think that the first step is to get to know people who have different cultures and skin colors," Mommy said. "I think it is also important to truly believe we are all equal as human beings. The last step is to believe that it is not ok to be mean to someone who looks different," She said with a smile.

"Mommy, do you think the man on the news is going to be ok?"
I asked. "Let's hope that he will recover soon and get his justice,"
Mommy replied. "Do you think anyone is going to hurt one of us?"
I asked with tears coming to my eyes.
"I do not think you have anything to worry about sweetie,"
Mommy replied. "Mommy and daddy are here and together to
protect you and your brother". She said.

"What can we do to help people heal from the germ?" I asked. "I think that it is important for you be proud and love the skin you are in. You should also show your friends that it's cool to have diverse friends," Mommy replied. "I can do that," I said with a yawn. "We have a deal!" Mommy said with a smile before she kissed me goodnight and turned out the lights.

- THE END -

Note to Parents:

The Germ is a book that will help you begin a healthy discussion with your child about racism and police brutality. Even though the subject matter is heavy, this is the reality of the world we live in today. This book does not give scholarly definitions of racism, because children can digest those more complex theories when they are older. Hopefully this book will help children understand that we are all equal, and we can ultimately all get along.

Deidra A. Sorrell

Discussion Questions

1.   In this book, racism was explained as a germ. Do you think the attitude of racism is a germ or a permanent condition?

2.   Have you ever experienced racism or prejudice (someone disliking you or denying your personal rights based on the color of your skin)?

3.   Have you ever felt negatively toward someone else based on the color of their skin?

4.   Have you ever harshly judged someone based on their appearance, country of origin, native language, accent, assumed lifestyle or assumed social economic status?

5.   What do you think is the cure to end the attitude and system of racism?

6.   What do you think is the way to end prejudice or the attitude of bigotry?

Pledge

I _____ pledge to learn more about people who are different from me (e.g. race, skin tone, culture, language) and reject treating others negatively because of racism or other forms of prejudice.

Signature & Date

Praise for

<u>Jaylen and the Green Book Reloaded</u>

Available at Amazon.com

"This book could save a young life."

-Amazon Customer

"Dr. Sorrell did a great job educating youth with this book."

-V. Tarlton, Author

"Beautifully written."

-Jay

CPSIA information can be obtained
at www.ICGtesting.com
Printed in the USA
LVHW071322160620
658247LV00015B/1136

9 781522 804383